Love and Such IV
A collection of poems

Ramona Powell-Poole

Love and Such IV

Ramona Powell-Poole

ISBN: 9798691715808

Cover image and design: Fiverr

Ramona Powell-Poole

Table of Contents

Ramona Powell-Poole

Ramona Powell-Poole

Acknowledgement

I give praise and honor to God for giving me the ability to express my thoughts and feelings during my time of sadness and bereavement.

To my accountability partners, I couldn't do this without you: Jujuana Howard, Ann Marie Bryan, Elizabeth Williams, Waletta Mason Dunn, Margo Thomas, Angela Hodge and to the entire (Tallahassee) Christian Authors Network (CAN) for their guidance and support, I greatly appreciate all of you.

Ramona Powell-Poole

This book is dedicated to my brother, Minister Lavern Powell. When I received the news that you were back in the hospital, it took me to a place where God ministered to me like never before. This book was written in three days. I love you, and I miss you daily.

Ramona Powell-Poole

Introduction

Love and Such IV (book 4 of 6) is a collection of poems about love, life, grief, and such. It contains poems, letters, and words of encouragement that were written during a time of great sadness and isolation. Any similarities to anyone or anything is just a coincidence. These poems are written in a variety of poetic styles. I hope that they will comfort you, help you cope, and bring you hope and peace as they do for me. Enjoy!

Ramona Powell-Poole

In the arms of the Father

I'm going to miss you, dear friend. Your struggles are over, and you're resting in the arms of the Father.

You gave me strength as I watched you fight a good fight. You always had a smile on your face even when I knew you were in pain. The doctors walked away from you many many times, but God said, "Not Yet." He gave you strength to overcome time and time again.

You have won many battles in your life and the victory is now yours. You can now say once again, "I'm doing something y'all haven't done; I'm resting in the arms of the Father."

"Oh, don't be jealous, your day will come and you will get to where I am. So until then live your best life, run your best race, finish your course, and then you can join me on the other side."

Thank you dear friend for sharing this space, you have taught me well. You've taught me things to do and things not to do. You reminded me time after time that it is our choice and those choices come with consequences.

Ramona Powell-Poole

You've taught me to love, you've taught me to share, you've taught me to never give up. You said, "Remember, God has the final say. Man is not in control, but it is God. I'm not leaving here until God gets ready for me and when He's ready; there is nothing anyone can do."

So, my friend, you left us with so much to remember you by and we will never forget. You will always be a presence in our lives. We loved you then and we love you now. We'll see you again dear friend, when it's our turn to be in the arms of the Father.

Ramona Powell-Poole

Believe

God made salvation so plain that even a fool could not error.

Accept that you need Christ in your life.

Believe that Jesus is the son of God and that He died and rose from the grave for your sins.

Confess it with your mouth that Jesus is Lord.

The way to Christ is so plain that even a fool cannot error.

Ramona Powell-Poole

You can do this

You can do this, no need to fret
You can do this, I'd make a bet
You can do this, just remind yourself
You can do this, you're the best!

You can do this, I believe in you
Don't beat yourself up, just start anew
Shake it off, pick yourself up
When all else fails, refill your cup.

You can do this, I believe in you
Plan your work and work your plan
Reevaluate your work and begin again.

You can do this!

Ramona Powell-Poole

Butterflies

Butterflies black and blue
Butterflies I see you
Pollinating like you do
Butterflies I see you

Butterflies orange and black
Butterflies please come back
Butterflies of pale hue
Butterflies in light blue

Striped like a zebra fluttering by
Butterflies up in the sky
Painted lady and swallowtails
Sitting on the fence post nails

Butterflies pink and blue
Butterflies I love you

Ramona Powell-Poole

Because He lives

Because He lives, I know I can face whatever life throws at me.

Because He lives, I know that I can do whatever needs to be done.

Because He lives, I know that He has my back.

Because He lives, no weapon formed against me shall prosper.

Because He lives, I can conquer any mountain.

Because He lives, I am strong enough, wise enough, brave enough, and powerful enough.

Because He lives, I am enough.

Ramona Powell-Poole

That's what love will do

When you love someone, you will put his or her needs before your own.

When you love someone, you will pray for them more than you pray for yourself.

When you love someone, you will do things that you never thought you had the strength to do.

Why? Because that's what love will do.

Ramona Powell-Poole

You're right

If you don't think you can, and you refuse to try

If you don't think you will win, and you refuse to fight

If you don't think you should, but don't bother to ask why

Then most likely you won't, and you're absolutely right.

Ramona Powell-Poole

Birds on the line

One bird two birds
Red bird blue bird
All in a row on the telephone wire
One on the ground next to my car tire

Yellow canary, I don't think he belongs
He must have escaped, but what a beautiful
song

The mockingbirds sing whatever they've heard
They are a copycat of other songbirds

Early in the morning they are my alarm
I hope they stay up high, out of the way of harm

The cats are below watching the line, hoping one
will fall so they can pounce in time

One bird two birds
Red bird blue bird
All in a row on the telephone line
Chirping and singing all at the same time

Ramona Powell-Poole

One day

One day I'll think, "How would I feel if all I believed was not for real?"

One day I'll talk about nothing in fact, then realize that I'm all off track.

One day I'll drive on a specific path, and then realize that I turned down the wrong path.

One day I'll bite a forbidden fruit, only to realize that I need to regroup.

One day I'll see that all of my wrongs have been forgiven, and my sins are gone.

One day I'll wait for that train to come in, only to see that it's gone, my friend.

One day I'll do what's on my list, do that job and fix that fix.

One day, I'll surely do all of the things I've wanted to.

If I keep on waiting, one day will come, and then I'll realize that one day is gone.

Ramona Powell-Poole

Time clock

Tic toc time clock time to go to work
Tic toc time clock time to go to class
Tic toc time clock time to go to church
Tic toc time clock time to go to mass

Tic toc time clock time to get a treat
Tic toc time clock time is going fast
Tic toc time clock time to dance to a beat
Tic toc time clock time to make it last

Ramona Powell-Poole

A change is coming

Hold on, a change is coming.

Be strong, a change is coming.

Don't give up, a change is coming.

Don't give in, a change is coming.

You can make it, a change is coming.

You can take it, a change is coming.

Lift your head, a change is coming.

Stick out your chest, a change is coming.

God's got your back, a change is coming.

Just stay on track, a change is coming.

It won't be this way always, a change is coming.

Ramona Powell-Poole

I'm drawn to you

Like a moth to a flame, I'm drawn to you.

Like a bee to a flower, I'm drawn to you.

Like an ant to a crumb, I'm drawn to you.

Like a dry plain to a storm, I'm drawn to you.

Like sand to a wave, I'm drawn to you.

Like light is to day, I'm drawn to you.

Like darkness is to night, I'm drawn to you.

Like coffee is to cream, I'm drawn to you.

Like metal to a magnet, I'm drawn to you.

Some things in life just belong together, so I
guess that's why I'm drawn to you.

Ramona Powell-Poole

Sunrise Sunset

Sunrise sunset, the beginning and the end, but what you do in the middle is what's important, my friend.

We all have to start, and there surely will be an end, but what you do in the middle is what's important, my friend.

The sun will rise in the morning and will set at night, you've got to get up and get busy; don't let the day pass you by.

All of our days are numbered; no one knows when they will end, sunrise to sunset, but what you do in the middle is what's important, my friend.

Ramona Powell-Poole

Trust God in all things

When you can't see your way, trust God.

When you don't think you can make it through the day, trust God.

When friends turn their backs, trust God.

When someone's bags are packed, trust God.

When it's out of your control, trust God.

When the truth hasn't been told, trust God.

When the pain won't quit, trust God.

When there's no time to sit, trust God.

In all the things you do, trust God.

Ramona Powell-Poole

Stormy weather

Drip drop the rain is falling
Swish swash the sounds are calling

Get inside or you'll get wet
Soaked to the core is what I bet

No umbrella needed
The wind took it away
It's going to be a dreary day

Lighting flashing
Thunder roaring
I can't even do my chores

Sit down and be still
That's all I can do
Too terrified to move
And too creepy too

Yes, I'm afraid
The clasps are loud
Like a winner cheering
To be heard by the crowd

The skies are dark
Look at how the wind blows
I wonder if it can rain
At the same time it snows

Ramona Powell-Poole

Love and Such IV

There it goes again
The thunder pounds
It's raining so hard
I can't even see the ground

The flashing is bright
The walls begin to shake
The thunder makes it feel
Like a small earthquake

The rain is pouring
Will it ever stop?
The garden is loving it
It'll produce a great crop

Drip drop the rain slows down
It's now taking longer
To hit the ground

The sky is clearing
The sun is coming out
The storm is over
The squirrels are running about

Ramona Powell-Poole

My Father can

My Father can be whatever you need Him to be.

Do you need Love?

Do you need Joy?

Do you need Peace?

Do you need Hope?

Do you need Help?

Do you need Clarity?

Do you need Direction?

Do you need Salvation?

Do you need Healing?

Whatever you need or can't understand, just remember that my Father can.

Ramona Powell-Poole

Bright eyes

Bright eyes bright eyes
Flickering like fireflies

Dancing around from here to there
Moving about without a care

Bright eyes bright eyes
How beautiful you are
Like the stars in the sky
You're twinkling from afar

Bright eyes bright eyes
How bright can you be
Can you light up the night
So that I can see

Bright eyes bright eyes
Flickering like fireflies
I hope you never forget
How beautiful you are

Bright eyes like fireflies
Tucked away in the jar
I hope you never forget
How beautiful you are

Ramona Powell-Poole

On the wings of a dove

One day you were here with me and now you are gone. You left on the wings of a dove.

I can feel you near me and I feel your love. You left on the wings of a dove.

I hear a whisper in my ear or a poke on my arm, I look around expecting to see you, but you are not there. You left on the wings of a dove.

A sweet fragrance in the air or a tug on my shirt, but you are not there. You left on the wings of a dove.

I long for your touch because I miss you so much. One day you were here with me, and now you're gone, because you left on the wings of a dove.

Ramona Powell-Poole

Don't judge me

When you look at me, you may see my pain, but don't judge me.

When you wonder why I do what I do, don't judge me.

When you hear me cry out like a cat in the night, don't judge me.

When I don't respond the way you think I should, don't judge me.

When I don't say the things you think I should say, don't judge me.

We all handle life differently. I'm not you and you are not me. Instead of judging me, pray for me.

Ramona Powell-Poole

Flicker Flicker

Flicker flicker went the light
The only thing I see tonight

The darkness is thick the air is thin
I'm scared to death like I'm in a pen

I can't breathe I'm terrified
I can't see I need some light
The power is out it's getting hot
What can I do
What have I got

I lit a candle it's getting low
And now my light is about to go
Flicker flicker went the light
The power's back on
I now have sight

Ramona Powell-Poole

A Note from the Author

Thank you so much for reading Love and Such IV. I hope you enjoyed reading it as much as I enjoyed putting it together. Please take a moment to share your thoughts in a review on Amazon or Goodreads. Long or short, it will be greatly appreciated.

About the Author

Ramona Powell-Poole is an author, teacher, and inspirational speaker who has been writing and delivering inspirational messages since 1986. She has used her upbringing in a Christian home to help channel her love for Christ and her desire to be an inspiration to all. She loves sharing her life experiences to show that no matter what life throws at you, you can overcome and prevail.

Ramona Powell-Poole

Please follow the author on Amazon

Check out other books by this author:

In the morning when I rise, 31 days of inspirational reading

Love Trust Live

Love and Such, A collection of poems

Website: www.ramonapowellpoole.com

Facebook: Love-Trust-Live Community

Love and Such IV

Ramona Powell-Poole

www.ingramcontent.com/pod-product-compliance
Lightning Source LLC
Chambersburg PA
CBHW072143150726

48002CB00004B/1612